MICROPOLIS

MICROPOLIS

THE ADVENTURE OF JOHNNY REDBLOOD

CORY MERTES

ARPress
45 Dan Road Suite 5
Canton MA 02021

Hotline: 1(888) 821-0229
Fax: 1(508) 545-7580

Ordering Information:
Quantity sales. Special discounts are available on quantity purchases by corporations, associations, and others. For details, contact the publisher at the address above.

Printed in the United States of America.

ISBN-13:   Softcover   979-8-89356-295-8
            eBook   979-8-89356-294-1

Library of Congress Control Number: 2024903677

CONTENTS

Cheer
S

CHAPTER 1

SARAH AND THE CITY OF MICROPOLIS

Sarah is a very cheerful ten-year-old year girl with long blond hair and several freckles on her cheeks. For her, today is an important day. After all, it is the start of summer vacation, and to celebrate, she and her mom are going to the nearby beach.

This is actually one of Sarah's favorite things to do, as she has grown up near the water and spends most of the warm summer days along the coast. Without a doubt she is excited about this trip and can't wait to get going.

As the morning sunshine peeks through her window, Sarah wakes up and rolls out of bed. "Time to get ready," she says to herself. "My new beach clothes must be somewhere in my room."

Sarah is good at finding things and shuffles through several piles of clothes. First, she uncovers her bathing suit and shorts. Then she finds a pair of sandals hiding in the back of her closet. Eventually, she locates everything she needs and proudly proclaims they really weren't missing.

Sarah gets dressed and runs downstairs for breakfast. She arrives in the kitchen and greets her mom with a big smile and shows her the new bathing suit that she is wearing. "When can we leave?" Sarah promptly asks.

Her mom is clearly amused and jokes that it is a bit early even for the fish in the sea. At the same time, she isn't surprised because Sarah has been looking forward to this trip for several months. In fact, over the years it has become their unique way of "starting summer" or, as Sarah points out, "ending the school year." After so many fun trips to the water, it just seems appropriate to begin their vacation this way.

As a special treat, Sarah's mom even got up early and made breakfast. There are pancakes and eggs, orange juice, and a bowl of fresh blueberries on the kitchen table.

Sarah is overjoyed. "What a perfect way to start the day," she tells her mom. Pancakes are one of her favorite foods, and the blueberries were picked from their garden and couldn't be better. With such a great-tasting meal, it doesn't take long for her to finish eating.

Sarah now suggests that the fish are awake, and her mom laughs that, yes, they probably are. The two of them pack a bag for the day which includes beach towels, sunscreen, and a new waterproof camera. In all, this is going to be a great day, and they leave the house for the short walk to the ocean.

It takes several minutes to arrive at the hiking trails that overlook the crescent bay and its crystal blue water. At this point, Sarah can smell the ocean air and see the waves crashing on the large black rocks which surround the tide pools. With each step, her heart rate increases and her whole-body tingles with anticipation.

This is where our story really begins, because within Sarah is a tiny city that is known as Micropolis. It is situated under a sunset red sky and filled with different types of single-celled creatures that live and work together. Overall, it is considered the nerve center of life and it plays a vital role in what Sarah does and how she feels.

The city, much like any large community, has several tall skyscrapers and smaller buildings to support its residents. It then extends outward to a beautiful lake of pure water surrounded by mountains. Beyond them are enormous canyons and long valleys with calcium deposits and other minerals. All of these areas are connected by a superhighway of electrical current. This roadway is called the "Artery Express" and it starts in the city of Micropolis, loops around, and eventually returns.

Along this highway are many different businesses, but one in particular is very important. This is the O.D.S., which stands for "Oxygen Delivery Service," and its purpose is to transport vital supplies to the people of town. To accomplish this, the company hires red blood cells to drive along the network of roads and drop off small canisters filled with oxygen. At the same time, they pick up used ones with carbon dioxide and return them to a processing plant to be refilled.

This is quite a job as the city is large and growing at an incredible rate. Due to this expansion, the company is constantly hiring new drivers, updating its maps, and working with the construction teams that are always in need of supplies.

With so much activity, the O.D.S. has to carefully schedule its drivers. Not enough oxygen can damage an area, but too many drivers might cause an accident. In all, Micropolis is a wonderful place that depends on many people to work together.

CHAPTER 2

BREAKFAST AT EMILY'S CAFÉ

Johnny Redblood and his best friend Ashley are two individuals that live in the city of Micropolis and work for the Oxygen Delivery Service. They can be easily recognized with their round, rose-colored faces and good-natured personalities. In fact, the only real difference between them is Johnny's short, spiky hair compared to Ashley's long ponytail. Other than that, they, along with the other red blood cells, are quite similar to each other.

Both Johnny and Ashley enjoy their jobs at the delivery company and look forward to any new place they can go. As a special treat, this morning they are having breakfast at a recently opened restaurant that everyone is raving about.

This is Emily Enzyme's Café, which is located on a small hill in the center of town.

Johnny and Ashley arrive at the same time and park their cars on the street across from the cafe. Although they haven't been here before, this place is easy to find because it has a huge sign on top of the building that includes the name of the restaurant "Emily's Café" and a colorful rainbow. Not only that, but the rainbow ends in a pot of gold appropriately located above the front door.

Emily's Cafe
Emily's Cafe

The two of them enter the restaurant, which is very busy, and are greeted by Emily Enzyme. "Good morning," she says in a cheerful way. "Just the two of you?"

Ashley replies, "Yes, just me and Johnny."

Emily walks them to a corner booth which overlooks Central Park. As they sit down, she hands them a menu and notes that "Today's Special" is blueberry pancakes topped with whipping cream. These are very delicious, and the berries arrived this morning.

Johnny thinks this sounds great and he orders the pancakes. Ashley also considers them but decides on scrambled eggs, toast, and orange juice. She does, however, order a side of blueberries, which seem to be very popular.

As they are waiting for their food, Johnny mentions that today he is going to Ankle Ridge, which is far from the city. He asks Ashley if she knows any shortcuts to the area.

Ashley pulls out a map and shows him the southern route of the Artery Express, which is really the only way to get there. She explains that the highway will go past the lake that supplies the city with water and then up and down a mountain pass. Eventually the road straightens out for a long drive through the Calcium Valleys.

As they are talking, Emily delivers their food. When she does, Johnny can't believe the size of the pancakes. They are the largest ones he has ever seen and are topped with a mound of delicious blueberries and a stream of whipping cream.

Ashley's meal is a bit smaller and includes several scrambled eggs with slices of green apples. She also has two pieces of toast and a bowl of blueberries. Not as exciting as Johnny's but definitely one of her favorites.

Both Johnny and Ashley love their breakfast and are grateful for the good-tasting fruit, which only come once in a while.

CHAPTER 3

JOHNNY REDBLOOD AND HEATHER HEART

Johnny finishes his pancakes and needs to get going, as it is a long drive to Ankle Ridge. He also wants to get back to the city before nightfall, when the Artery Express slows down, and the overall trip will take much longer.

Johnny thanks Emily for breakfast, wishes Ashley well, and walks to his car. When he gets in, Johnny is happy because he is driving a brand-new vehicle.

His last car was so old that the tires were worn, and the supply racks were loose. On several trips, the oxygen canisters would rattle and break, making the delivery fairly useless. As such, the older vehicle was turned in and he was given a brand-new one.

This car, like the previous model, is a red-and-white convertible with four wheels and a backseat for carrying passengers. It also has a spacious trunk for the oxygen tanks and a decal that depicts the skyline of Micropolis on each of the side doors.

For power, the vehicle uses a small battery and a tank of oxygen similar to the ones they deliver. Both are placed under the hood and can be easily recharged at the Central Power Station. When the car is moving, it creates a small amount of "oxygen exhaust," which helps deliver the resource to other parts of town.

Johnny is very excited about his new car. He leaves the city limits and merges onto the Artery Express, which is running fast this morning. As such, it doesn't take long to pass by the lake and traverse up the mountain pass.

When he gets to the top of the hill, Johnny has a great view of the city on one side and the lower valleys on the other. In fact, he can even see the Power Plant, which is located on a remote island. To access the facility, there are several long bridges that cross over the water.

As he gets closer to the station, Johnny hears the routine beating of the equipment. It has a fairly soothing sound. In all, it thumps at a steady pace, not too slow and not too fast.

Johnny, like most of the other red blood cells, is amazed at how this small complex creates the power for all of Micropolis and the superhighway. He wishes he could stop by and see Heather Heart, who runs the station. Unfortunately, his trip will take most of the day and he doesn't have any extra time.

CHAPTER 4

DOWNTOWN MICROPLIS

Back in the cafe, Emily asks Ashley how she liked her breakfast. "Everything was great," Ashley replies. She wants to stay and talk but it is getting late, and she needs to start her deliveries.

Ashley thanks Emily for the delicious food, gets in her car, and heads to the center of town. On the way, she passes two of her favorite parts of the city.

First there is the Central Gardens. This is a section of the park that seems to get bigger and more vibrant each day. Once in a while, plants die, but they are soon replaced by another flower or tree that is typically larger and more colorful than the last one. Right now, the garden is doing well, and everything is in bloom. It is really an inspiration to the people of town.

The second location is the Library of Knowledge. This building is one of oldest and tallest structures in the city, but it is overloaded with books. In fact, it typically doubles in size every year and a construction team is constantly working on it. Fortunately, the mayor left plenty of room to expand the space.

Ashley passes both these places and arrives at her first pick-up located on the corner of Main Street and Eye Street. She stops at the recycling bin, which is well marked with an O.D.S. decal, and gets out of her car.

Ashley opens the bin and takes out all of the used blue canisters filled with carbon dioxide. She loads these into the trunk of her car and replaces them with new red ones filled with oxygen. Immediately the bin turns from blue to red to signify that, new canisters have arrived and are available for use.

Later on, the surrounding stores, which include an aroma shop and a visual broadcasting center, will stop by and take the canisters for their operations.

During the day, Ashley will replace the tanks at a number of stations throughout town. When all of her new canisters are gone, the "red" on her car will turn "blue." Everyone will know that her new tanks are gone, and she is returning used ones to Larry Lungs Processing Plant, which is next to the Oxygen Canyons.

CHAPTER 5

THE BLACK SEA URCHIN

Sarah and her mom have a pleasant walk from their home and arrive at the shoreline. When they get to the beach, it is windy, so Sarah's mom puts her daughter's long blond hair into a ponytail. When she does, Sarah tries not to complain, but she is somewhat impatient and can't hold back a dissatisfied facial expression.

Her mom is not amused but realizes that her daughter is doing the best she can. Overall, the whole routine would be much easier if Sarah would stop bouncing up and down with excess energy.

When her mom finishes, Sarah runs to the warm water of the Pacific Ocean. "Finally," she says to herself and looks back with a big smile as if to say "Thanks, Mom." Sarah plays in the calm water until she reaches the far end of the protected cove.

Here there is a row of shallow black rocks that form a section of tide pools. More importantly, they contain a variety of miniature sea life.

Sarah looks around and finds several interesting things. First, she notices a family of crabs on the outer edge of the rock formation. As she watches them, the crabs get swept into the water by a small wave and then scurry back to the rocks seeking shelter. Sarah considers this a fun game of "hide and go seek."

Besides the crabs, there are colorful starfish and green sea plants that dance in the water as the "ocean current" comes and goes.

With so much going on, Sarah takes out her camera for a few quick pictures. Right away, she snaps a photo of a fish as it appears to be stuck between two large shells. Another picture includes a hermit crab who clearly looks amused at the large stranger with the funny black box.

Later on, Sarah finds a colorful starfish partially hidden behind a tall, bushy sea plant. As she focuses the camera, another wave comes in and Sarah loses her balance. Her next step is not on the soft white sand but on a black sea urchin, which has several long, sharp needles.

One of these punctures her foot, and it starts to bleed.

"Ouch!" she yells, as the injury is very painful and unexpected. Sarah hobbles back to shore. When she gets to her mom, Sarah points to her ankle and explains what happened.

"Oh, my goodness," her mom says. She can't believe how swollen it has become. Sarah's mom feels terrible about the injury and tries to clean the wound with some water and a cloth from her purse. She eventually gets her daughter's foot to stop bleeding and covers the area with a Band-Aid.

During this time, in the lower valleys of Micropolis, Johnny Redblood is making his way to Ankle Ridge. Everything is going well until he hears a thunderous noise and a huge, black needle jets through the wall of the superhighway and smashes into his vehicle. Johnny is thrown from his car as it tumbles over and over before it comes to a stop.

"What in the world was that?" he says to himself and is completely shaken by what just happened. He gets up and is shocked to see an immense black object stuck in the roadway. Then, he looks to his left, where his new car is completely banged up and resting on its side.

"Oh no," he says. Sammy Salt, the delivery manager, is not going to appreciate the damage to his vehicle. Overall, Johnny is lucky to be all right, as the sharp needle caused an enormous amount of damage to the outer wall and roadway.

For starters, there is a gaping hole to the outside world, and water quickly fills the roadway. Then several cars aren't able to stop and crash against the large black object. Other vehicles are sucked out of the opening and disappear from sight.

Within minutes, there is a huge traffic jam; the pointy needle is completely blocking the roadway, and no one can get through.

In the midst of this confusion, Johnny observes three green thugs leaving the black object. He hears them talking about the accident and they seem rather amused at the destruction the needle has caused. "That was awesome," one of them says. Another one replies, "Look at all the smashed vehicles and the saltwater flooding in."

These not-so-friendly intruders carry a bag of supplies, so apparently, they are planning on staying awhile. One of them is taller and more menacing than the others, and he seems to be the leader of the group. He is called "Tyrus the Virus" by the other two people.

After they joke about the situation, Tyrus and his two friends leave the urchin and walk down one of the side streets. In all, the only evidence of their arrival is an unpleasant odor and a green slime that their footsteps leave behind.

Johnny can only guess their intentions, but they appear to be looking for a hideout, hoping that no one has seen them.

CHAPTER 6

THE TRIP TO THE WASTE FACILITY

Several construction workers, who were building roads nearby, are called to the site of the injury. When they arrive, the crew starts to remove the black needle from off the Artery Express. To do so, they attach long lines of rope to the object and use all their might to slide it across the road.

Slowly but surely the workers pull the heavy needle from the highway and out of the opening. Now that it is gone, they make a temporary patch of the hole that will at least stop the water and dry air from pouring in. In a few days, a specialized team of repairman will install a permanent replacement.

For the rest of the day, the construction workers clean the area and fill the gash in the highway to make it drivable. When it gets late, they prepare to leave but schedule another crew to come out in the morning and finish the job.

Johnny, who stayed around to help, shows one of the workers his damaged vehicle and asks for a ride back to Micropolis. This individual, whose name is Curtis, can give Johnny a lift, but it will take several hours to return to the city. First, he has to drop off the trash bags at the Waste Disposal Site and then his van needs service at the Central Power Station.

Johnny understands and is very thankful for the help.

The two of them get into Curtis' vehicle and travel up the Artery Express. When they reach the Lower Midlands, Curtis takes an underground passageway that leads to a desert crater surrounded by steep, rocky cliffs.

In the middle of this crater is a two-story, redbrick building the Waste Disposal Site. It is certainly one of the largest structures around and seems bigger when you consider the tall chimneys on each side of the location.

Since it is late at night, nobody is around, and Curtis parks the van near the front of the building. They get out of the vehicle, pick up the trash bags, and walk slowly to the main entrance.

As they enter the building, there is a huge circular fire pit with a couple of tall, bright flames. "Now that is big," Johnny says, as the fire is significantly higher than he is and almost reaches the top of the two-story building.

Curtis jokes that they should have brought a few marshmallows. "Just a few," Johnny says, as those flames could roast marshmallows for the entire delivery company. They laugh at each other; they haven't eaten in a while, and the marshmallows definitely sound good.

They continue past the fire pit to the far end of the room where there is a moving conveyer belt. Johnny and Curtis place the trash on this platform, and it is carried to a small opening in the wall. It then slides down a vertical shoot, never to be seen again.

Johnny asks Curtis where the trash goes. "Well," Curtis replies, "I don't really know," and then somewhat jokes that "once it is gone, it is gone, and that's about it." Sounds good to Johnny. Overall, the two of them are just happy to get rid of the trash.

Curtis and Johnny leave the disposal site, which is actually kind of smelly, and return to the van. They drive to the other side of the desert crater, passing a murky lake and waterfall.

Their next stop is the Central Power Station, where they can service the van.

CHAPTER 7

HEATHER'S FACILITY

Curtis and Johnny continue on the Expressway until they reach the bridge that connects the mainland to Heather Heart's power plant. At this junction, Curtis changes lanes and drives over the water to the tropical island where the electrical station is located.

Curtis enters one of the tubes and parks the van in a temporary holding area. The two of them get out of the vehicle and walk to the cafeteria. As they do, they see a large group of people in one corner of the room. This is somewhat unusual, as it is late at night. Johnny explains that the accident probably used a lot of oxygen and now the drivers have to recharge their vehicles. He also notes that Heather Heart is over there. He can tell because Heather is easy to spot. She, unlike anybody else, has a more "human" appearance, with sand-colored skin, long blond hair, and stunning blue eyes. Overall, Heather is a very unique person, and she typically has the latest information on the city.

As they approach the group of people, Johnny sees Ashley. He calls her name, and she turns around.

Ashley is very glad that Johnny is all right. She knew he was near Ankle Ridge when the accident occurred and that many drivers were either hurt or got washed into the open air. She gives him a hug and asks, "How are you doing?"

"I am lucky to be here," Johnny replies with a smile. "The needle that crashed through the wall also hit my car, and I was thrown from the vehicle. I have a few bumps and bruises, but my new car is completely wrecked. Because of the damage, I had to get a ride back with a construction worker." He points to Curtis, who is standing next to him.

Johnny also tells her about several germs he saw leaving the black needle. They were certainly up to no good.

Ashley knows the new intruders could lead to a serious infection. Since it appears that Johnny was the only one to see them, she offers to take him back to the city, where he can update the mayor.

Curtis and Johnny look at each other and neither can argue with Ashley. Curtis prefers to stay and get some rest, but Johnny is worried about the three intruders from the black needle. They decide that he should return with Ashley and the sooner the better. "Let's get going," Johnny says.

He is actually glad to spend time with Ashley, but it has been a long day. Johnny says good-bye to Curtis and gets into Ashley's car.

She drives the vehicle to an exit tube, and the inner door closes. At this point, the chamber fills with air, which recharges the battery and the oxygen tank. When the outer door opens, the car is launched from the tube by a large puff of wind. This is similar to a roller coaster that is shot down a hill or a musician blowing air through a flute.

On their way back, Johnny and Ashley recount their busy day and how breakfast at Emily's seems like such a long time ago.

CHAPTER 8

TYRUS THE VIRUS

The three intruders Tyrus, Grim, and Clyde lived on the urchin a long time, and they are happy to leave that miserable place. The urchin, with its long black needles, was cold and dark, and they were confined to a small area with not much to eat and not much to do.

To Tyrus' surprise, this new place is warm and spacious, with plenty of locations to explore and opportunities for adventure. He just needs to develop a plan, and a few more followers would help. He's hopeful that some people who live here might be persuaded into joining him. After all, Tyrus can be a very intimidating creature with his gruff looks and dominating personality.

His two other friends, Grim and Clyde, are similar to Tyrus but shorter and rounder, and they don't have the motivation of their leader. "Just happy to be off the urchin," they mutter to each other.

The three of them explore a few areas and find a remote location that is great for hiding out. In addition, there is a damaged vehicle with several oxygen canisters that are completely full. They are grateful to have these supplies, which will last for several days while they get used to their new surroundings.

ODS OXYGEN
ODS OXYGEN
ODS OXYGEN

As they walk around, Tyrus notices that their footsteps leave dark spots of goo that melt the ground into a green slimy liquid. They all think that this is quite an unusual substance.

With not much to do, Tyrus picks up a handful of the green mud, rolls it into a ball, and throws it against the wall of the superhighway. This small amount of goo explodes upon impact and then each tiny piece grows into a larger area of dead burnt matter. This stuff is clearly destructive and quite entertaining.

Grim and Clyde join the fun and toss mud balls around their campsite. This causes a lot of damage, but they eventually get bored. "What should we do next?" Grim says.

Tyrus, who would rather keep them busy, suggests they create a mud slick on the superhighway to see what happens. "Okay," the two of them say. Grim and Clyde pick up the mud and move it to a section of the Artery Express.

Right away the gooey liquid bubbles up and melts the road. It gets deeper and deeper until a large mud pit forms that covers a section of the highway.

Soon thereafter, a delivery car comes along and tries to get through the green goo. However, it is too deep, and the vehicle gets stuck in the mess. The driver puts the car in forward and reverse, but the tires won't budge. The driver has no other option but to abandon the vehicle and return to the city.

Tyrus, Grim, and Clyde are very proud of themselves. "That was great," Grim says and Tyrus laughs. He had no idea the goo could trap a car.

They walk to the vehicle and open the trunk. Here they find several full oxygen tanks. "What a pleasant surprise," Tyrus says, and they take the canisters to add to their supply of tanks.

Later on, a construction van arrives to clean up the mess and tow the vehicle back to the city. When it leaves, Tyrus and his friends shovel mud onto the highway, and the whole process starts all over again.

CHAPTER 9

THE GERMS

One afternoon while Tyrus, Grim, and Clyde are throwing the slimy goo against the walls of the superhighway, two desperate characters approach them looking for help. They introduce themselves as Floyd and Rex and explain that they are germs who were badly beaten by the city's troops. Thus, they have a scruffy-looking appearance.

Tyrus is interested and asks what happened.

"Certainly," Floyd says. Several days ago, he and Rex were looking for food and decided to sneak into the city of Micropolis. In the middle of the night, they passed the gates of town and thought they had entered the city unnoticed. However, within minutes they were approached by security guards.

"What are you doing here," the officer said. Rex replied that they were getting supplies for the lower valleys and had traveled all day. Apparently, the guards didn't believe the story and thought they should go to the station for more questions.

Floyd and Rex refused to leave, and the police officers started to arrest them.

The two germs had no other option and fired several bacteria balls. Unfortunately, these shots just bounced off the officer's protective armor and fell to the ground. "That's not good," Rex said and hoping to get away, they ran down a side street.

As expected, the police followed and launched arrows of white plasma. These shots hit the germs, and they started to bubble up and dissolve. That was a rather painful experience.

Before they were hit again and completely dissolved, the germs found an entrance to the city's underground sewer system. They climbed down this opening and lost the officers in one of the many tunnels.

Floyd and Rex stayed in the sewers for several days until they ran out of supplies. At this point they were forced to walk along the highway looking for help.

Tyrus and his friends appreciate the information, as they didn't know anything about the city or the troops. They assumed the delivery cars came from somewhere but had no idea it was a large, well-protected city. Tyrus thanks the germs for the story and offers them some oxygen.

Floyd and Rex are grateful for the supplies. However, they really want to join Tyrus and his friends, who seem to have a good hideout and plenty of oxygen.

Tyrus listens to their request, but he doesn't think they have much to offer and asks the germs to go.

As they are leaving, Floyd walks past the mud slick, which he knows is fairly destructive. Hoping for some good luck, he picks up a handful of the goo, covers his hands, and shoots a bacteria ball coated with the slimy green mud. To everyone's surprise, the ball is launched farther than they have seen before.

It flies down the road, crashes against the wall of the superhighway, and dissolves this section of the road into a puddle of water.

"That was really impressive," Tyrus says. He knows that Floyd and Rex have something valuable to offer, and he asks them to stay.

CHAPTER 10

THE WATER CANAL

Tyrus decides to recruit more germs that can use the green mud. To do so, Rex mentions there is a hidden city which includes a number of infections that were defeated by General White and his police force. Some of these germs might be willing to join them.

Tyrus agrees but wonders, "If the city is hidden, how do we get there?"

"I have a map," Rex replies, and he pulls out a wadded piece of paper that he found in the sewers. Floyd laughs and says that this could have come in handy when they were lost in the tunnels or trading for oxygen. Nevertheless, he is glad they have some directions.

The germs examine the map and find the location of the hidden city, which is right next to the waste disposal site. They also realize that a central river runs throughout the area and ends at a lake next to the city's entrance. "How convenient," the germs say and "We can just take the river."

Tyrus, who seems to be the only one with any common sense, mentions that they don't have a boat and they certainly can't swim.

Grim, who is usually very quiet, has a solution. When they arrived, he found a vehicle that was badly damaged from the urchin's needle. He pulled it aside and repaired it to a reasonable working condition. Although it has a few dents and scratches, they can drive it to the river and then it will float down the canal.

They all like this plan and get into the vehicle.

As they make their way to the river entrance, Grim sees another delivery car approaching from behind. He turns around and fires a mud ball at the vehicle. "Good shot," Rex says as the slime hits the front of the car and explodes upon impact.

Pretty soon all of the germs are launching mud balls at the vehicle, and several more hit their target.

The driver of this car is completely surprised by the attack. He has no choice but to jump out of the vehicle before it dissolves into the ground or bursts into flames.

"That was fun," Floyd says, and the germs look for another vehicle to shoot at. Unfortunately, they are the only ones around and have to launch their mud balls against the walls of the highway. Overall, they appear to be causing a significant amount of damage.

Before long, Tyrus and his friends hear the rushing water of the canal, and they know it must be close. They follow the sound of the river and park the car on a service road next to the riverbank.

Tyrus isn't sure if the vehicle will float, so he tells everybody to get out. All of the germs follow his advice and exit the vehicle. Then, they roll the car over the edge and into the water. The car makes an enormous splash, but sure enough, it stays upright, floating in the river.

They get in and down the canal they go. To their amazement the path never seems straight. They are either turning right or left, and occasionally the flow of the water is so great that it pushes them up the side of the river. When this happens their boat almost flips upside down, which will certainly drown them all.

"Hold on tight!" Tyrus yells to his friends. Grim, Clyde, and the two germs can barely hear him; the rushing water is loud, and it echoes against the ceiling of the canal. They all know this wasn't the best idea, but they can't turn back.

The river continues to move in every direction until they plunge down a steep waterfall and land in the lake next to the disposal site. For now, the river is calm as it slowly flows into the facility.

CHAPTER 11

THE HIDDEN CITY FOR GEMS

Tyrus and his friends can't believe they made it in one piece, and they get out of the car. In addition, they are lucky that it is early in the morning, and nobody is here.

They look around and Floyd locates a small round lid that appears to be out of place. It is stamped with the letters "GHRT," which stands for "Germs Have Rights Too." This is the unofficial motto of the city and certainly the entrance they were looking for.

One by one they walk down a ladder to a smelly, dark place with a very high ceiling. When they reach the bottom of the stairs, they find a small community of shops on a street that loops in a circle. At a quick glance, they can see a restaurant, an ice-cream parlor, and a bowling alley. All of these places are very busy.

Rex and Floyd point out that there are many types of germs in the underground city, and some have unique talents. For example, there are germs that can make the temperature rise, while others can multiply and block the essential roads of the city. There are even germs with jackhammers that make deep cracks in the ground.

General Store
GermCity
General Store
Flu's Ice Cream
PARLOR
Flu's Ice Cream
PARLOR
Germ City
General Store
Germ City
General Store

All of them have been defeated by the security guards and are in pretty bad shape. To be fair, they really didn't have a chance, and most will stay in the underground city until they completely dissolve. Others might try to escape through the waste disposal facility, but nobody really knows where this goes.

Tyrus, who is the most dominating of the group, is introduced to these germs. He explains how he arrived from a sea urchin when one of its needles punctured a hole into their land. In addition, he and his friends can make a slimy green mud, which is very effective against the city's troops.

At first the germs don't care much for these outsiders and pretty much ignore them.

To get their attention, Tyrus fires a mud ball down the street. This small amount of goo flies through the air and explodes against a trash can, which bursts into flames. Rex then fires a shot at a streetlamp, and it promptly dissolves into a puddle of water.

After this display of destructive power, the germs are willing to listen.

Floyd gets out a bag of mud and shows them how to coat their hands with the slimy green liquid. In doing so, they are able to launch a mud ball with the same devastating effect. Once the germs realize they have a fighting chance against the police, all of them volunteer to join Tyrus and his friends.

This is good news for Tyrus, who now has an army of followers. He decides to return to their hideout, where they can manufacture large quantities of mud to supply all of their new friends.

To get back, Tyrus and the other germs follow the underground sewer system. This will keep them safe until they reach an opening near their campsite. Then, there is a short walk along the Artery Express.

CHAPTER 12

CARLOS CRANIUM

Back in the center of town, Carlos Cranium, the mayor of Micropolis, is in his office eating a blueberry muffin from Emily's Enzyme's cafe. He always enjoys Emily's restaurant, but today she has outdone herself with the excellent pastries.

As he finishes eating, there is a knock on his door. It is General White, who is in charge of the police officers and the security force for the city. "Good morning," he says to Carlos and asks if they can talk about the injury at Ankle Ridge.

"Most certainly," Carlos replies. He expected General White to show up at some point during the day.

The mayor explains that the accident affected two important parts of the city. The first was the Central Power Station. For several minutes, it was running at full capacity. In fact, the pumps were going so fast they almost ran out of supplies.

The second was the Oxygen Canyon. There was so much panic that air wasn't coming in, and they were practically empty. This made it impossible to refill any of the tanks.

Luckily, the construction team arrived and was able to quickly push the object out of the opening. At this point, Carlos called Heather Heart

to slow down her pumps, and everything seemed to calm down. When this happened, the Canyons started to refill with air.

General White is amazed at how fast things fell apart. He is glad that everything is back to normal but wants to know more about the strange object that broke through the superhighway.

"Yes, of course," the mayor says. He has a report from the construction team which includes several drawings and a summary of what happened.

Carlos shuffles a few things here and there and locates the reports, which were somewhat hidden in a pile of papers. In all, he has to be good at finding things, as his office includes stacks of paper from all the important parts of the city. One day he will try to organize it, or at least he intends to.

Together they review the reports and think of ways to prevent another injury from happening.

CHAPTER 13

JOHNNY'S UPDATE

During this time, Johnny and Ashley arrive at the mayor's office, knock on the door, and enter the room. The mayor is surprised to see them, but he knew Johnny was in the area when the needle punctured the highway.

Carlos asks Johnny how he is doing and if any of his friends were hurt. Johnny replies that he is well, but several other drivers were washed out of the opening. Unfortunately, there wasn't anything he could do about it.

"I'm sorry to hear that," Carlos responds. He hoped to prevent such an incident, but this was completely unexpected. The mayor asks Johnny if he has any more information on what happened.

"As a matter of fact, I do," Johnny replies. He explains that he saw three germs leave the dark black object. They were large and green, and their footsteps left behind a slimy liquid that seemed to burn the ground.

Needless to say, the mayor and General White are alarmed at the news, as neither of them knew anything about these germs. "Do you know where they went?" the general asks.

"No, they just disappeared down a side street," Johnny replies.

General White and Carlos look at each other and wonder what to do. They need to find these germs and decide to form a search party. Since they are not familiar with the area, General White asks Johnny and Ashley to come along.

The two delivery drivers agree to join them, but they need to get permission from Sammy Salt, the delivery manager at the O.D.S.

"Very well," General White says, and the three of them make their way to the delivery company.

CHAPTER 14

SAMMY SALT AND THE O.D.S.

Johnny, Ashley, and General White arrive at the O.D.S. garage. They enter the building and look for Sammy Salt, who is usually easy to spot. After all, he is the only one that is not a red blood cell, and he somewhat resembles a large white popcorn ball.

Not surprisingly, they find him in his office working on the schedule for the day. "How is it going?" they ask. Sammy is glad that Johnny survived and responds that it has been a hectic day; many drivers and cars were lost in the accident. He has everyone working overtime and then he's had to reroute the cars around the injured area.

Sammy asks Johnny about his encounter with the needle. "It was very close," Johnny says. In fact, his vehicle was hit by the object and rolled many times. "No worries," Sammy replies. "It can be replaced, and I already ordered a number of vehicles for the ones that were damaged. Let's just move forward from the accident and try to prepare for next time."

General White explains that he is going to Ankle Ridge to look for three intruders from the black needle. He would like Johnny and Ashley to come along and help with the search. He also assures Sammy that they will be well protected with his best troops.

Although Sammy is short-handed, he thinks this is a good idea. Something strange is happening in the lower valleys, and he tells them about the unusual mud slicks and the stolen canisters.

General White is now even more determined to find these intruders and asks Sammy if there is anything else he can do. "Are you able to take extra supplies?" Sammy asks, as the injury and stolen canisters have caused a shortage of oxygen in the area.

"Of course, we can," General White says. His army trucks have plenty of space in the back.

Shortly thereafter, a group of police officers arrive at the O.D.S. They are driving large white army trucks with a picture of the Micropolis skyline and the police force's motto, "To Protect and to Destroy." Clearly, they take their job seriously. Then, several more officers arrive on motorcycles that will follow the caravan of cars.

Sammy wishes them well, and the small group of vehicles, led by Johnny and Ashley, leave the garage for the trip to Ankle Ridge.

CHAPTER 15

SARAH'S HEALTH

Although it has been several days since Sarah stepped on the sea urchin, her foot is still sore, and the swelling has only partially gone down. Besides this, every now and then, black spots appear near her ankle and last for several hours. Overall, she is feeling sick and tired.

This is discouraging, as summer just began, and Sarah is missing the fun with her friends.

At the same time, Sarah's mom is concerned about her daughter. She thinks that Sarah should be doing better, and the black spots, which grow like spiderwebs, are very strange. She makes an appointment to see her doctor, who can hopefully provide an answer to this illness.

Cheer

CHAPTER 16

THE GERMS RETURN TO THE HIDEOUT

Tyrus and his friends leave the waste disposal site and travel the underground sewer system. It takes a while, but they finally exit the tunnel near their old hideout. When they do, Tyrus notices that the area is dark and slimy with several large cracks and potholes. At the same time, there is green mud dripping from the ceiling and forming a river of goo in the middle of the road.

Clearly, the mud is more destructive than they originally thought.

As they walk along the darkened expressway, a construction van covered in slime approaches the large group of germs. It is out of control and narrowly misses the germs before it crashes against the side of the highway and bursts into flames.

The driver slowly gets out of the vehicle and appears to be shaken up. He is then hit with a mud ball that was fired from one of the germs. This construction worker, who is usually a light shade of yellow, turns into another creature that is lime green and consumed with mischief.

This is quite a surprise to Tyrus and his friends, who had no idea this would happen.

The construction worker joins the germs and provides important information about the city of Micropolis. He explains that the town and all of its residents depend on Heather Heart and the Central Power Station.

If the germs can take over this facility, they will control the electrical current for the highway and the power to the city. Then, they can force the mayor to step down, and Tyrus will be the new ruler of the land.

"That is a very good idea," Tyrus says, but right now he needs to find more oxygen tanks. After all, with so many germs, they will run out of food in a day or two. If this happens, they will dry up and dissolve into the ground.

Therefore, when the large group of germs reach their hideout, they immediately create an enormous mud pit to trap several delivery vehicles and steal their supplies.

As they finish shoveling the slimy liquid onto the road, Johnny, Ashley, and General White come along the highway. They encounter the large mud pit that Tyrus created, and their vehicles immediately get stuck in the mess and stop dead in their tracks.

Tyrus and his friends didn't expect this caravan of vehicles, and they panic at the sight of the troops. In response, the germs launch as many mud balls as they possibly can.

General White is the first one to exit his car. When he does, several green projectiles hit him. The mud dissolves his protective clothing, and he turns into one of the lime-green creatures. The general's new appearance is shocking, and he joins the enemy.

The other troops exit their vehicles and launch new fire bolts which strike several of the germs. Although the city's police put up a good fight, they are outnumbered and no match against the germs with their new supply of mud. One by one they are hit and turn into the lime-green creatures of Tyrus's army.

Ashley and Johnny are surprised at the scene the troops have never been defeated. Without any protection of their own or ability to fight back, they decide to return to the city. The two of them jump on the motorcycles, which had stopped before the mud slick, and leave the area. As they do, several slime balls are fired, and one unlikely shot strikes Ashley. She is knocked off her bike.

She turns into a green monster and stays behind.

Johnny is heartbroken. He has just lost his best friend, and now both she and the leader of the troops have joined the enemy. Johnny knows this is the work of Tyrus. He recognizes the green mud and the smell from his first encounter with the intruders.

What he hadn't expected is the large following that Tyrus has and the destructive nature of their slimy green goo. He must find a cure for this new virus, and it has to be soon.

CHAPTER 17

AN UPDATE FROM CARLOS

Johnny gets back on the motorcycle to leave Ankle Ridge, but the Artery Express only goes in one direction. Therefore, he has to take a couple of side streets before he can return to the freeway going in the right direction.

When he does, Johnny is amazed at the amount of damage to the road. There are cracks and potholes everywhere, and in some areas the slime is so thick that he can barely get through. To an extent, these darkened tunnels look like a giant spiderweb of goo.

Due to these poor driving conditions, it takes the rest of the day before Johnny reaches the outskirts of town and the headquarters of the O.D.S.

When he gets back, Johnny parks the motorcycle outside the garage and enters the building. Right away he notices Sammy Salt and Carlos Cranium working together with several maps of the area.

Johnny approaches them and explains the terrible outcome of their trip. When he is finished, Sammy and Carlos are astonished. They can't believe that the general, his troops, and Ashley are all gone, and worse yet they have become part of the enemy.

Sammy and Carlos tell Johnny that the rest of the city is also under attack. They explain that the green mud is everywhere. In fact, it is causing an unbelievable amount of damage to the roads and is spreading to the buildings and the water supply.

They also believe that other germs are helping Tyrus, as the temperature is rising, and the Oxygen Canyons are filling up with water.

Lastly, there is concern for Heather Heart and the Central Power Station. She has been working hard to keep the expressway moving at its typical speed. However, with all the damage, her equipment might slow down or even stop working.

The mayor can't believe it, but the city is falling apart.

Emily's Cafe

CHAPTER 18

THE HEALTH CLINIC

As they finish their conversation in the garage, Sammy Salt notices a small amount of goo stuck to Johnny's motorcycle. The three of them examine the dried mud, which appears to be too small to cause any additional damage.

Carlos asks Johnny to take the specimen to Dr. Marcia Marrow at the Health Clinic. The mayor knows that if anyone can find a cure for the illness, it will be Marcia. He will contact Emily Enzyme, who can meet them in the lab and help with the work.

Johnny puts the dried mud in a glass container, gets on the motorcycle, and races to the Health Facility. When he arrives, Dr. Marrow is waiting for him.

She takes the glass container and thanks him for bringing the mud. Marcia explains that it isn't easy to get a good sample. Sometimes a specimen is too small to examine. Other times it is too large and dangerous to handle. She thinks this is the perfect size.

They go upstairs to her lab, where she places the mud under a microscope and carefully examines it. Marcia concludes that the green slime is a defense for the black needle that pierced the wall of the superhighway. Even under the microscope, where it is perfectly safe, she notices it trying to melt the glass container in which it is placed.

She believes that this reaction is similar to the motives of the three intruders. Although there is no need for them to defend the needle, they have a destructive nature and are creating damage for their own pleasure and survival. She has not seen this particular substance before but believes that a remedy can be found.

At this time, Emily arrives and brings several boxes of fruits and vegetables from her restaurant.

Marcia takes these ingredients and places them on her table along with a row of colored bottles. She explains that the liquids in these glass containers have healing properties that can be used against the germs. For example, there is an orange one, which is carrot based, a green one, which is spinach based, and a purple one, which is a combination of blueberries and strawberries.

When there is a new germ attack, she combines several of these nutrients until the right formula is created that will be effective against the invaders.

Under Marcia's instruction, they mix the items together until it forms a dense liquid that is opposite the color of the mud and its underlying properties. Dr. Marrow now believes they have a substance that can destroy Tyrus and reverse the effects on their friends.

She fills a bottle with the new solution and proceeds to the troop's headquarters, which is located next door. As she enters the building, a group of police officers are coming back from the valleys and are covered in the green slime. Dr. Marrow sprays them with her new formula.

The solution turns the mud bright yellow and then it evaporates into the air.

"Perfect," she says. She and the troops are relieved that this new remedy is effective. Dr. Marrow runs back to the lab to inform Johnny and Emily.

CHAPTER 19

THE CITY'S DOWNFALL

Sarah is starting to feel very ill. She has a high temperature, and each breath is forced and restricted. But most of all, her foot has not healed from the accident with the urchin. It is red and swollen with black lines that run up her lower leg.

Although it has only been a few days since she stepped on the spiny needle, her injury is severe and only getting worse.

Sarah's mom is also concerned, and her dad leaves work early to see how she is doing. When he arrives home, Sarah's dad can't believe how sick she has become. He knows that an urchin's sting can be harmful, but nothing like this. He asks her how she is feeling, and Sarah responds that she could be doing better and that this is not the best way to start her summer vacation. Her parents can't wait any longer and take her to the nearest hospital.

When they arrive at the medical center, the doctor admits Sarah and examines her ankle and lower leg. He explains that sea urchins have poison that can spread throughout the body. This infection can be treated, but it will take time to completely heal the wound. The doctor prepares a shot that will help reduce the effect of the urchin's sting. He also assures Sarah's parents that this is the best way to cure her illness.

Back in the Lower Valleys, Tyrus jokes with Grim and Clyde that their plan is coming together. They were fortunate that the caravan of cars that carried the troops had a large number of oxygen tanks. This gave them the resources they badly needed.

Right now, everything is in place for an assault on Heather Heart. Not only have they increased the size of their army, but they created a large mud slick to supply the troops.

This river of goo flows down one side of the Artery Express and forms a small lake. It is then channeled into a factory for the production of mud balls and protective shields. The mud balls are easy to create, but the shields take a bit longer. For them, the workers have to heat the goo with the germs that can raise the temperature and then mold the liquid into hard surfaces that can deflect the fire bolts from the city's troops.

In addition, Tyrus is using several germs that have unique talents. For example, there are germs that can clog the roads of the city and others that can pollute the air and water. However, most of the germs are trying to collect as much oxygen as possible and to convert the residents into the lime-green creatures.

As a result of these ventures, Tyrus has created much damage on Micropolis and its surrounding areas.

Overall, he is ready for the final assault. They get into several vans stolen from the construction workers and repainted green and travel up the Artery Express.

CHAPTER 20

MAURICE AND THE M-TROOPS

The Micropolis police, who are now led by Major Star, have been busy helping the construction workers repair the damage to the city. However, they can only do so much and are focused on the more critical areas of town. This includes the water reserves and the air in the Oxygen Canyons.

Both of these resources have been polluted by the germs and their endless supply of green mud.

Major Star has assigned some of his troops to these important areas, but he also knows that Tyrus will make a final push into Micropolis and will pass by Heather Heart's facility. Thus, he takes all of his remaining troops to protect the Central Power Station.

As the troops arrive at Heather's facility, they set up a protective circle around the outer edge of the tunnels leading to the inner chambers. They need to ensure that Tyrus doesn't enter the facility and cut off the pumps. If this happens, the city will be without power, and the superhighway will come to a complete stop.

While Major Star is setting up his defense, Johnny, Emily, and Dr. Marrow successfully make large quantities of the solution to combat the infection. As they complete a batch, it is poured into an empty oxygen tank. Later, they load all of these canisters into a construction van, which is fairly spacious and has several large racks for carrying supplies.

With Johnny driving, the van leaves the health clinic and starts its journey to Heather Heart. Emily and Dr. Marrow also make the trip and are in the back of the vehicle with the canisters.

As they travel along the Artery Express, another needle comes piercing through the outer layer of the highway and almost crashes into the van. This occurs as Sarah's doctor gives her a medicine shot to help fight the urchin's poison.

Luckily, Johnny slams on the brakes, and the van comes to an abrupt stop just before it hits the needle. In doing so, Dr. Marrow and Emily are thrown forward and end up next to Johnny in the front seat. "What is going on?" they ask him. Johnny shows them the large needle blocking their path. He can't believe it. He almost got hit a second time from an object that sliced through the wall of the superhighway.

The three of them get out of the van to inspect the long needle.

As they look around, a number of troops and vehicles come pouring out. They are about the same size as the red blood cells but are dressed in brown army uniforms. Better yet, their vehicles are rugged jeeps and will have no problem with the cracks and potholes in the road.

The leader of these troops is named Maurice, and he explains that their mission is to find and destroy an illness that was caused by a sea urchin's poison.

Johnny is thankful for the help and explains that they, too, are heading for the germs that have caused so much damage and are now threatening to take over the city. He tells the new troops that he can lead them to this infection and its leader, Tyrus the Virus.

Johnny also shows them the new solution they created, which is effective against the green mud. He is bringing this substance to Major Star, who is leading their troops and is protecting the Central Power Station.

Right now, it is a race against time.

CHAPTER 21

THE BATTLE FOR HEATHER HEART

Tyrus and his army reach the bridges that lead to the Central Power Station and Heather Heart. Here he can see that the police force has assembled a large number of troops and have several long-range catapults for the battle.

As the two forces approach each other, Major Star yells "fire," and hundreds of glowing white balls are launched from the catapults. These shots enter the red sky above the bridge and come crashing down in the middle of Tyrus's army.

Although several germs are hit and start to dissolve, most of them remain safe under the protective shields they recently created. Tyrus's troops endure volley after volley but continue to march forward.

When the troops from each side get closer, lightning bolts are launched from the police, and mud balls are fired from the germs. As these two projectiles cross in midair, numerous collisions occur, and the green mud explodes upon impact. In doing so, there is small fireworks show, and most of the lightning bolts are damaged and fall helplessly to the ground.

However, the mud balls break into smaller pieces and continue on their way to the city's troops. These projectiles land on the catapults,

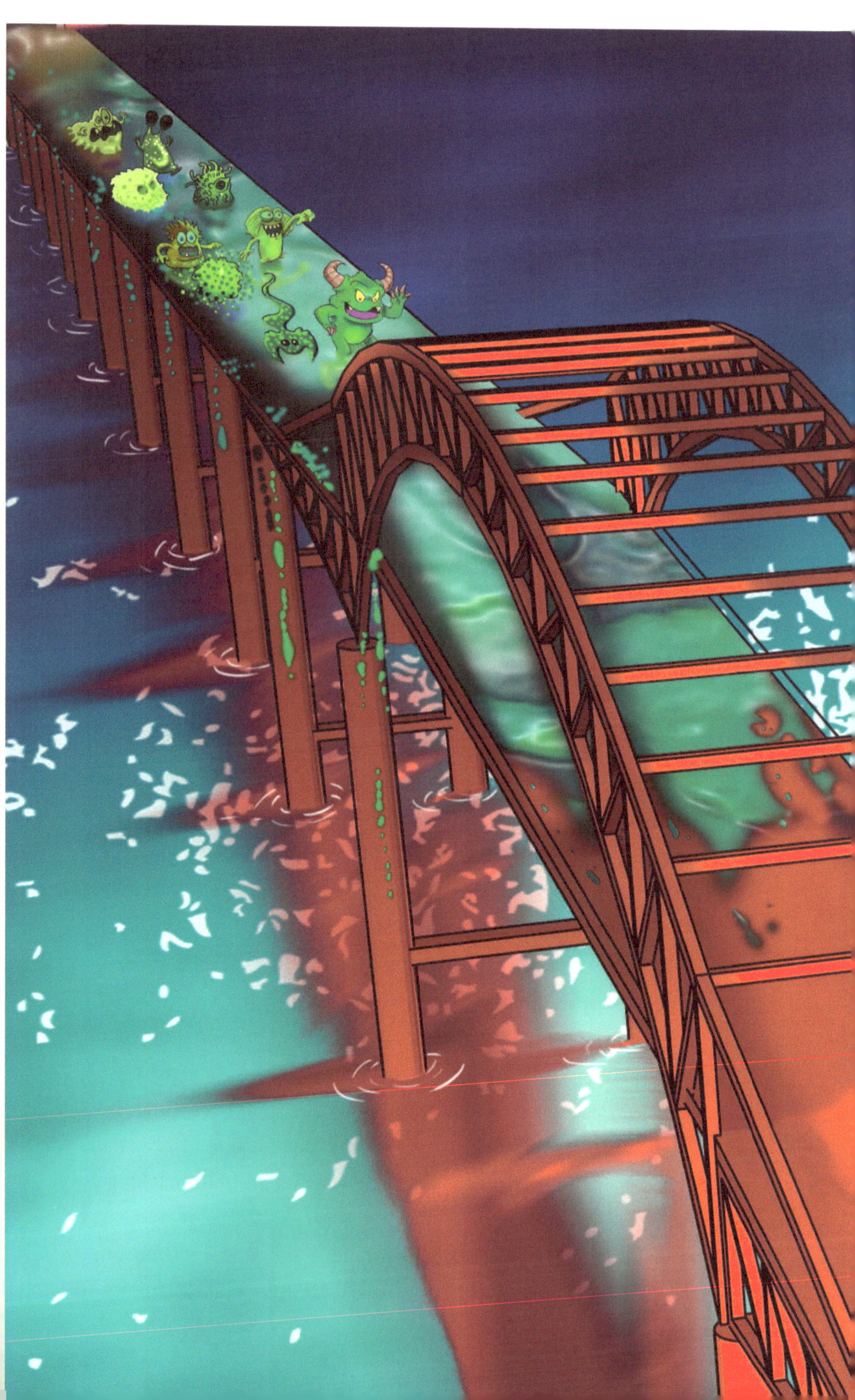

which then burst into flames and burn to the ground. At the same time, other mud balls hit the police officers, who turn into the lime-green monsters of Tyrus's army.

Because of the damage and loss of troops, Major Star is forced to retreat into the tunnels of Heather's facility. Here he can reassemble his remaining officers in the large open space of the control room. At this point they can attack the germs as they exit the tunnels. This will be their last chance at stopping the infection.

While this is going on, Johnny and the M-Troops approach Heather Heart's facility. They can see the damage being inflicted on the police, and Johnny knows he has to reach Major Star before it is too late.

Right now, this is going to be difficult because the germs are situated between him and the city's defenders. Johnny considers several options and comes up with a very good plan. He will leave the M-Troops, and they can attack the infection from the bridges leading into the station. Johnny and his friends will take the van to an exit bridge where there is a valve that does not completely shut. He can squeeze the vehicle through this opening and then drive into the control room.

Johnny, Emily, and Marcia leave Maurice and head to the exit bridge.

As he is driving, Johnny thinks about Ashley, who was turned into a lime-green monster and joined Tyrus's forces. As much as anything, he wants to save her and return them to their normal lives. With these thoughts, he continues as fast as he can to the exit bridge where he can enter the facility.

Johnny crosses the southern entrance of the Central Power Station. Once here, he leaves the superhighway and continues on the exit bridge. About halfway down he stops at a lookout point that is shielded from the oncoming electrical current. If he gets any closer, the force of the charge is so great it will push him over the edge of the bridge.

Johnny carefully waits for the electrical current to pass and then he drives the van to the valve that doesn't completely shut. He squeezes the vehicle through the opening and drives to the control room.

As they enter the chamber, everyone is amazed and glad to see their friends.

Johnny notices that Heather and Carlos are busy working the controls, while Major Star is positioning his troops for the final battle with Tyrus. They greet each other and Johnny shows them the new liquid that can dissolve the green mud and destroy the infection.

He also explains that new troops have arrived, and they will be fighting the germs from the bridges leading into the facility.

Major Star is thankful for the solution and the risk they took to deliver it. He and his officers unload the new substance and place the canisters next to their troops. Immediately they dip their hands into the liquid for the battle against the germs.

The timing is perfect as the first wave of Tyrus's army comes through the tunnel.

The police officers launch their new fire bolts at the germs. These shots go straight through the shields and dissolve the germs into puddles of water.

Tyrus notices that his troops can't advance any farther, but he is determined to take over the power facility. He continues to send in germs, but each wave of troops is met with the same volley of fire bolts. The new solution has a devastating effect on his army.

Meanwhile, Maurice and the M-Troops attack the germs from the incoming bridge and have similar success.

Tyrus and his followers are caught between these two forces with nowhere to go. Their numbers are dwindling, and only the lime-green monsters remain. As these germs are hit, the new formula turns them back into their original selves.

During this time General White joins Major Star for the final assault. They have pushed the infection from the control room to the incoming bridge where Maurice and his troops are approaching from the other direction.

As a result, it doesn't take long for the massive army of germs to be reduced to just a few individuals, including Tyrus, Grim, and Clyde.

Tyrus knows that his time is up. His army has been defeated, and his plan to take over the city is lost. He surrenders to General White and Major Star.

CHAPTER 22

THANKS TO ALL

The mayor is very happy with the outcome of the fight and proud at how hard everyone worked together to save the city. The mayor also thanks the M-Troops for their timely support and invites them to stay in Micropolis.

After several days, the construction crews finish the repairs to the superhighway and the connecting bridges. Besides the roads, the temperature is back to normal, and the water and air, which were polluted from the germs, have been cleaned. In all, Micropolis is doing quite well.

As the city returns to normal, so does Sarah. She had spent several days in the hospital and is glad to be home. Right now, she appreciates her mom's home cooking and even looks forward to another day at the tide pools.

Overall, this was an experience for Johnny and Ashley. They are exhausted but happy to be together. Tomorrow, they are even planning a trip to Emily's Café, where hopefully they can find some hot pancakes and fresh blueberries.